Acknowledgment
The publishers would like to thank John Dillow
for the cover illustration.

Ladybird books are widely available, but in case of
difficulty may be ordered by post or telephone from:

Ladybird Books – Cash Sales Department
Littlegate Road Paignton Devon TQ3 3BE
Telephone 0803 554761

A catalogue record for this book is available
from the British Library

Published by Ladybird Books Ltd Loughborough Leicestershire UK
Ladybird Books Inc Auburn Maine 04210 USA

About the
ZOO

by JACQUELINE HARDING
illustrated by MAUREEN HALLAHAN

Ladybird

We went to the zoo.
It was a big park
with lots of
different animals.

zoo animals

The lion cubs were playing games.

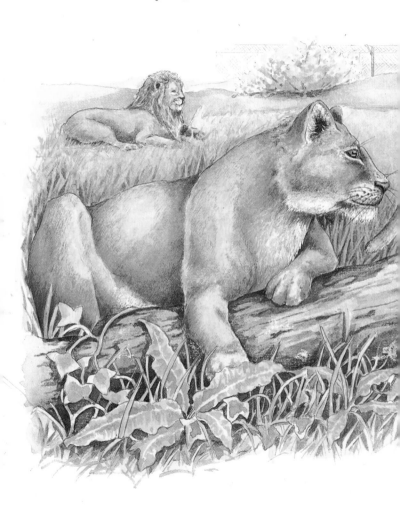

lion

The mother panda was
holding her baby.

panda

The giraffe looked
funny when it
bent down to
drink.

Do not feed Giraffes

giraffe

Here we could touch
and stroke the
animals. The rabbits
were hungry.

rabbits

The seal caught a fish
in its mouth.

seal

The leopards were
resting in a tree.

leopards

There were three enormous elephants and two babies.

polar bear

Then the gorillas
watched **us** having
a picnic.

Picnic
Area

gorillas